DORY GLORY

Building a boat
from stem to stern

written and photographed by

ANDREA MABEE

Bass Cove Books • Kennebunkport, Maine

Published by BASS COVE BOOKS
57 North Street
Kennebunkport, Maine 04046

ISBN 978-09630074-1-4
0-9630074-1-6

Book design by Cecile Bayon
Printed in USA by Edison Press, Sanford, Maine 04074

Acknowledgments

If one could give out an award for patience, two people, who happen to be related, would certainly each be presented with one. Ruth Fernandez, Matt's mother, always had a smile and a kind word, and Matt, my 10-year-old boat builder, was forever agreeable and never objected to my sometimes silly ideas. Both were patient beyond my expectations.

The Landing Boat School, in Arundel, Maine, which produces first-class boats and boat builders, deserves to be mentioned for its complete cooperation in granting me access to photograph this project even though I lacked any credentials that suggested that I knew what I was doing. Special thanks to Paul Barton for checking the technical accuracy of this book.

Claude Demers, Bill Koffler, Scott Massi and Dave Parker were superb for tolerating my presence while they diligently worked on building the dory. I'm sure at some point they were wondering if they were going to get extra credit for having to put up with me.

Many wonderful friends have also helped along the way reading and helping with copy editing. Two friends in particular are Susan Rouillard and Anita Matson whose professional skills were utilized to the max.

The porch where this story begins was generously made available to me by Glenda Lovell.

Thanks also goes to Kristen Faulkner for scanning my photos into the 21st century.

Joshua and Andrew, my own two sons, deserve recognition for having shared with me their passion for fishing and an appreciation for how important it is to own at least one or two boats.

A heartfelt thanks goes to my mom, Rita Zisser, for her stalwart support over the years while I have tried on and worn a variety of hats.

Lastly, great appreciation goes to my husband Carleton for always viewing everything, including this project, in such a positive light (even though he did suggest I rewrite the entire story as it was going to press) and for maintaining an "it can be done" attitude, even in the most challenging circumstances.

Chapter One
THE END OF A GREAT SUMMER

It had been a wonderful summer. Matt sat on the porch daydreaming about the foggy early mornings and bright glistening afternoons he had spent fishing off the docks and piers of the small Maine fishing village where he lived.

The highlight of the summer, however, had been the day spent on a charter fishing boat with his dad. When they boarded the boat, the captain told them that cod, bluefish and even some haddock had been caught earlier in the week. He said he couldn't make any promises, but he thought that more than likely they'd reel in something worthwhile. As it turned out, his prediction was correct. After fishing for almost two hours without a bite, Matt finally felt a tug on his line. Trying to keep calm, Matt did everything just right. On the second tug he gave the rod a strong jerk upward to set the hook. Repeatedly he let the line out and then gradually reeled it back in. When the fish had finally tired, Matt reeled in the biggest bluefish he had ever caught. What a LUNKER!

Unfortunately, fishing from a boat was something Matt rarely had the opportunity to do since his family didn't own one. To Matt this seemed incredibly unfair. Living so near the ocean and not having a boat didn't seem quite right. "Oh, well, with summer over and school starting tomorrow there won't be much time for fishing anymore," Matt thought regretfully.

That evening, before he went to bed, Matt prepared everything he needed to bring to school the next day. The carefree days of summer were over, and now it was time to get organized and stay focused on his school work. Matt would never admit it, but he was actually a little nervous about going back to school. Although he really wanted to do well, it seemed that no matter how hard he tried he just couldn't get good grades. It wasn't that he didn't like school, but it was just so difficult to sit still and pay attention.

The good news was, now that he was older, he would be taking some classes that sounded interesting. He was particularly curious about a technology class where the students designed and built projects like CO_2 cars. That was the type of hands-on project that Matt really liked. He also thought it was great that this year he was scheduled to eat during the first lunch session. Now he, as well as his classmates, didn't have to listen to his stomach rumbling like it did last year. That had been a little embarrassing! The first lunch session was also less crowded, so it would be easier to get a seat at a table with his friends. Having a chance to catch up with friends was definitely an important part of the school day. So, although Matt regretted the end of a great summer, there were some things he was looking forward to, at least that's what Matt told himself as he tried to fall asleep.

Chapter Two
OPENING THE DOOR

Happily for Matt, the first day of school went by smoothly. His teachers seemed really friendly, and some of them even made an attempt to be funny. It went by so quickly that he was amazed at the end of the day when the dismissal bell rang. On

his way home he decided to take a different route because earlier at lunch one of his friends had mentioned an interesting piece of news. An old barn had recently been sold and then completely renovated. What used to be an old cow barn was now a school for boat building. Since he really didn't have any reason to rush right home, he thought it might be fun to go "check it out."

When he stopped in front of the old blue barn, Matt was not sure he had found the right place. He looked up at the building. A sign over the door read "The Landing School," but when his eyes wandered to the side of the building, he saw another door with a hand-painted sign: DORY GLORY, TOP-EST, SECRET-EST BRAIN NEST. Cautiously, he approached the opened door and poked his head inside.

"This sure doesn't look like a boat school," Matt thought to himself. "There isn't a boat in sight. All I can see are people sitting, lying and kneeling on the floor, drawing on large white boards." Matt was disappointed. "There must be a mistake," he thought. "This looks like an art school, not a boat school." Just as he turned to leave, he heard someone ask, "Hey, can I help you?" Matt felt himself getting slightly red in the face. He realized that the man speaking to him had been standing on the other side of the doorway watching him. "No, I don't think so. I'm looking for a boat building school," Matt managed to answer sheepishly.

"Oh, well, in that case step right in, your search is over. I'm known around here as Dave. What's your name?" Although he was still slightly embarrassed, his curiosity got the best of him, and Matt introduced himself as he entered the barn.

"You're probably wondering where all the boats are," Dave said as if he had been reading Matt's mind. "Well, there aren't any boats here yet, but as an instructor it's my job to see that three are built by the time Christmas rolls around. Right now I've got to get back to my students. Please feel free to join me," Dave said, and without pausing he headed off to the other end of the barn. Matt followed right behind.

"So how's it going, Claude?" Dave asked, as he knelt down next to a woman who was leaning over a long white board. "I'm not sure I've gotten this curve right, Dave. I'd like you to check it," Claude replied.

Dave looked up at Matt and explained, "This is the first step in boat building. It is called LOFTING. When you loft a boat, it means that you are drawing the exact plans of the boat. It's really like a blueprint for a house except that the plans are the actual size of the boat. As for tools, all you need to draw the plans are some awls, a tape measure, a pencil, a T square and some wooden BATTENS to help you draw the larger curves." A batten is a thin flexible piece of wood. By drawing the plans full size, a boat builder can see the details of the HULL.

The hull is the main structure or body of the boat.

Two other students who were working on the same board came over to talk to Dave and then introduced themselves to Matt. Their names were Scott and Bill. "Hopefully, we'll draw these plans accurately, and in four months a dory will be sitting on this spot," said Scott. "Do you know what a dory looks like?"

"Sure I do," Matt said. "I've seen several of them in the harbor. A dory is a great boat. It rows well, sails beautifully, and best of all it's a great fishing boat."

"It sounds like you really know something about boats," Claude said, looking at Matt with a twinkle in her eye. "I bet you didn't know that dories have been used by fishermen in the waters off Canada and New England since the late 16th century." Then she turned to Dave and half-jokingly said that she thought it would be fun if Matt came by to watch them as they worked on their boat. Dave didn't respond right away but then to everyone's surprise exclaimed that he thought it was a great idea.

"At the end of the week we close the school early and everyone is in a hurry to leave. The shop is usually a mess. If you are interested in earning a little money, I could pay you to help us clean up, and you can see how we throw these boats together. Occasionally, we even need an extra pair of hands, and I imagine yours just might do in a pinch. What do you think?" Dave asked. "It sounds great to me," Matt said, "but I better check with my parents to see if it's OK with them. Sometimes they're a little funny about me doing things after school. They have this thing about school being a priority and how I need to make sure that nothing interferes with it. I'll have to convince them that this isn't going to take any time away from my studies. How about if I stop by tomorrow to let you know what they say?"

Drawing the curves

Chapter Three
WELCOME ABOARD

When Matt arrived home he could hardly wait to tell his parents about his visit to the boat school and Dave's job offer. To Matt's surprise, his parents thought that taking the job was a great idea. Matt's parents knew that their son really did well with hands-on projects and felt that this would be a great opportunity for him to observe people who were also talented in this area. They were also in favor of Matt accepting the responsibility of an after-school job. However, just as Matt had suspected, his parents said that they would only agree to let Matt accept this job if it did not affect his grades in school.

The only other concern Matt's parents expressed was about safety. Matt's mother had all sorts of questions about the kinds of power tools that were used at the boat school. In the end, Matt's dad decided that he would feel more comfortable if he visited the school and met Dave himself. Matt didn't really think this was necessary, but since it seemed to be the only way he was going to get the OK from his folks, he agreed to let his father stop by the boat school to check it out.

The next morning Matt's father left the house earlier than usual so he could stop by the boat school on his way to work. The students hadn't arrived yet so he had a chance to meet with Dave who assured him that his son would be well-supervised. Before he left he was given a tour of the school and was almost late for work because he found the place so fascinating. As far as Matt's father was concerned, this was a fantastic place to learn all sorts of interesting things about boats and boat building. In fact, he was so excited by what he saw that he called his wife as soon as he arrived at his office.

That evening after Matt reassured his parents that he would not neglect his school work, they finally gave him the go-ahead to accept the job at the boat school. As Matt and his father were going upstairs after dinner, Matt's mother overheard her husband tell Matt that he could certainly understand how excited Matt was about working at the boat school. His own childhood was filled with great boating memories, and he was delighted that his son seemed to have inherited a fondness and appreciation for boats. It was unfortunate that they didn't own a boat already, but he wasn't sure they could afford to buy a boat. Hopefully, though, sometime in the future that might change. Listening to their conversation, Matt's mother was delighted that her husband and son had an interest that they could enjoy together.

Later that night when Matt sat down to tackle his homework, he took out an extra notebook and decided that it might be fun to keep a list of all the new boat building terms and facts he would learn at the boat shop. At school one of Matt's favorite teachers had announced that she would be willing to give an extra-credit grade to any student who did an independent project. The project could be about any subject. The only requirements were that the student had to feel passionately about the subject and that he or she had to provide proof of having gained some in-depth knowledge of the topic.

At this point Matt really didn't want to add to his school work, but he thought that perhaps a project about boat building might not be too difficult. He figured that if he just added a few new words to his list each week then perhaps he could make it part of his project and it wouldn't end up being too overwhelming. He also knew from looking at his past report cards that any extra credit he could get would be very helpful.

"When do I begin?" Matt asked the next morning when he stopped by the school to inform Dave that he had hired a new worker. Dave extended his hand

and said, "Welcome aboard. It will probably take the students another week to finish lofting their boat, so why don't you stop by next week to see how they have progressed." Matt was a little disappointed that he wasn't going to start right away, but Dave explained that sometimes boat building is a slow process. He also said that the first lesson to learn was that to be a good boat builder you need to have a lot of patience.

Welcome aboard! ➤

Chapter Four
FROM STEM TO STERN

The week seemed to crawl by slowly, as Matt was anxious to begin his new job. "So what do you think of my masterpiece?" Scott asked when Matt came by exactly one week later. Matt turned in the direction that Scott was pointing and saw an elliptical-shaped board resting on top of two sawhorses. "It's great, but what is it?" Matt asked, hoping he didn't seem too ignorant.

"It's the bottom of the boat and it is made of pine. A narrow slit has been cut out of the middle so a piece of wood called the CENTERBOARD will be able to fit through it. Claude is working on the centerboard section right now if you want to see what that looks like."

Claude had overheard the conversation between Scott and Matt and motioned Matt to come over to where she was working. "The purpose of the centerboard is to help keep the dory

≺ *The bottom of the dory*

11

Drilling an opening in the centerboard

stable and on course when the sail is being used," Claude explained. It can be raised up into the boat or lowered into the water when it is needed. To make the centerboard heavier, a rectangular section of wood is cut out, and lead, which has

been heated up and melted over a fire, is poured into the space. Once the lead cools, it will harden and provide the centerboard with the extra weight that is needed for it to work effectively. There will be other steps taken before the centerboard can be considered finished. A waterproof sealant will be applied, and when that dries, it will be sanded and painted several times. These steps will be taken for many other parts of the boat as well, and none of these steps can be rushed."

Looking over at the long workbench, Matt was now observing Bill. "What's the section of the boat called that Bill is working on?" Matt asked Claude.

"That's the transom," Claude answered. The transom is the back end piece of the hull and it will be attached to the bottom of the boat.

≺ Filing the opening of the centerboard
where the lead will be poured

Planing the transom

Attaching the transom ➢

The back or rear section of the boat is called the STERN. To make the boat both strong and beautiful, the transom will be constructed out of mahogany. Mahogany is a hardwood that is often used for special sections of a boat. Bill is being very careful while he is working with this wood because it will not be painted, but only varnished, when the boat is completed. Surfaces of the boat that are left natural or unpainted so that you can see the wood are called the BRIGHTWORK. Well, we are just about finished for the day so don't let me keep you any longer. I'm sure you can't wait to tackle the job of cleaning up this place!"

Matt looked around the shop. "Yeah, there sure is a lot of sawdust. Next week try not to make such a mess," he said with a slight grin on his face.

During the following week, Claude, Bill and Scott were given the task of building four RIB FRAMES. The frames, which are made of oak, serve two purposes. The first is to make the boat more rigid, and secondly, they provide a surface for the PLANKS to be set upon. Once they are constructed, each one is attached to the bottom of the boat at a specific location. They are then checked and rechecked with a tool called a level to make sure that they are lined up exactly right. The planks are the boards that make up the siding of the boat.

When Matt returned at the end of the week, Bill was at one end of the boat attaching the transom while Claude was at the other attaching the STEM. The stem is located in the BOW, which is the front of the boat, and it is the piece of wood that fits in the space where both sides of the boat come together.

"The stem is sawn from one piece of oak," Claude explained to Matt while she worked on fitting it to the bottom of the boat. "When we start to plank the dory, the planks will be fastened from the stem all the way to the stern."

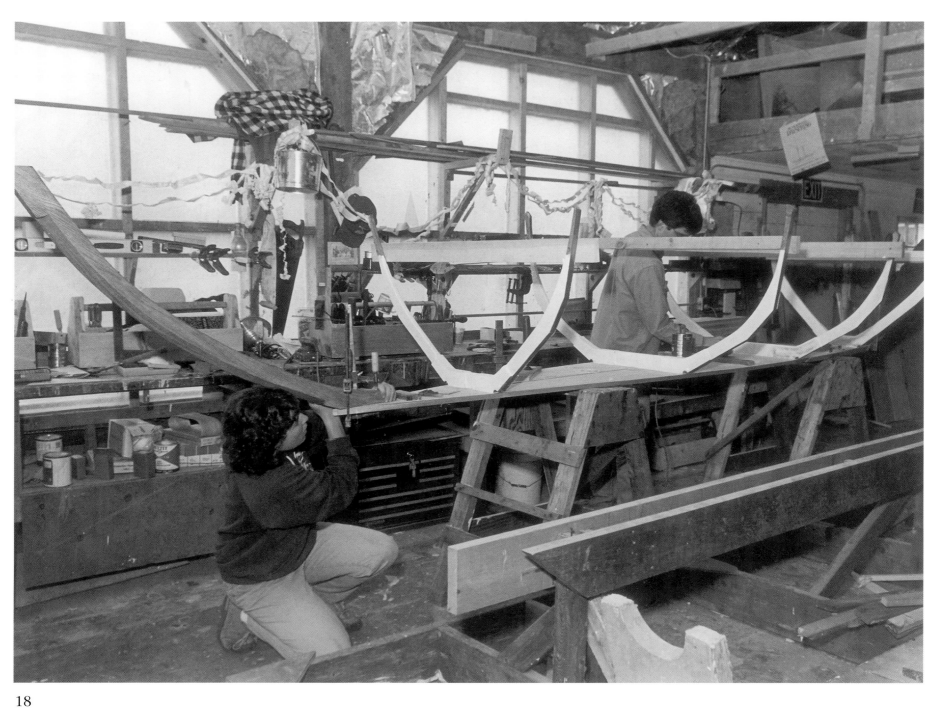

18

"It's beginning to look like the skeleton of some sort of prehistoric dinosaur," Matt said, as he walked around the boat.

"Well, I think the next time you see it, it is going to look a lot different because as soon as I fasten the stem on, we are going to turn the boat over and attach it to a STRONGBACK. The strongback is a structure that is designed to hold the dory up in a stable position so that the crew can work on the boat more easily without it moving," Claude explained.

For most of the following week, the students continued to secure the dory on the strongback and to make adjustments to the frames. Chiseling, shaving and sanding each piece of the dory are necessary in order to make all the pieces fit together perfectly like a puzzle.

◄ Attaching the stem to the "prehistoric dinosaur"

The strongback ⋏

Leveling the dory on the strongback ➤

21

Chapter Five
A HELPING HAND

When Matt arrived at the shop on Friday, Bill told him that the crew was hoping to begin fitting the first planks on Monday. "You could give me a hand by sanding the transom flush to the dory bottom," Bill said.

Matt was thrilled to be asked to work on the boat, so as soon as Bill gave him the sanding block he set right to work. By the time Matt was done with his task, the students were ready to leave, and he began his job sweeping up the shop. Every now and then Matt would stop sweeping, though, and glance up at the skeleton-like creature. "Would this really turn out to be a boat?" he wondered. At this point it was very hard to imagine the dory completed.

At home that evening Matt told his parents all about the progress of the dory. His enthusiasm was so great that his father suggested that he pick up Matt from the boat school on Fridays on his way home from work so that he could also have a peek at the boat. Matt thought that was a great idea since it was starting to get a little colder now that fall was turning towards winter. It was already getting dark, and he had to walk almost a mile to his house from the boat school.

Trying to keep his grades up, Matt was now staying after school once a week to get extra help. He also decided to take advantage of his teacher's offer and asked her if she would accept an extra-credit project about boat building. To Matt's delight his teacher said that a short oral presentation and a list of boat and boat building terms would definitely be acceptable as long as he met the most important requirement: He had to be passionate about his subject. She also asked Matt to have the project completed by the time the semester was over, which was the week before Christmas. Matt felt confident that he could meet all the requirements

Sanding the transom ➤

for this project. In fact he really had never before tackled an assignment with such enthusiasm. He had already begun a vocabulary list of boat building terms and was adding to it weekly. Although in the past he had usually felt uncomfortable about giving oral presentations, he decided that he wouldn't think about it for the time being.

On Monday Claude began making the GARBOARD PLANK. The garboard plank is fastened to the bottom of the boat and is made from thin pieces of plywood that are SCARPHED together. When two pieces of wood are scarphed, they are tapered so they overlap when they are joined together to form one piece. The garboard plank must bend over all the frames from one end of the boat to the other, or in boating terms, from stem to stern! Getting this plank to fit accurately requires a lot of skill and patience. When Matt arrived on Friday, he was surprised to find that the entire boat had not been planked yet. "Gee, I thought this vessel would be just about ready to put in the water," he said to Claude.

"Well, it's taken me a lot longer than I thought it would to fit this plank, but if it isn't perfect, you're bound to end up with a leaky boat," Claude replied. "It's a little tricky trying to clamp this plank on myself. How about holding it in place for me?"

After Matt finished giving Claude a hand, he decided to see what Scott was working on. He found him on the second floor of the shop gluing together two long narrow pieces of wood. "Right now I'm working on making a SPAR. A spar is a pole. When a boat uses a sail, it is rigged, or attached, to the spar. A boat that has a sail must have at least two spars, a vertical spar and a horizontal spar. I'm working on the horizontal spar which is called the BOOM."

"It looks as if you have a long way to go until this project is finished," Matt

Attaching the garboard plank ➢

25

*Clamping the
centerboard trunk case*

commented. "How are you going to turn this rectangular piece of wood into a round pole?"

"One step at a time," Scott replied. "Since there isn't much else that can be done to the boom until the glue dries, you might want to find Bill and see what he is working on." Scott didn't offer any further explanation about how he planned to turn the boom into a perfectly round pole, so Matt took Scott's suggestion and headed off to see what Bill was working on. Dave was right when he said that you needed to have a lot of patience to build a boat.

Bill had just clamped the CENTERBOARD TRUNK CASE to the workbench and was looking it over when Matt came by. "Hey, Matt, what do you suppose this piece does?" Since Matt had been in a sailboat before, he was pretty sure he knew the right answer. "It holds the centerboard in place when it's not in the water," Matt answered proudly.

Bill smiled and said, "You're right. I guess you really are quite the boatman after all."

Just as Matt had finished sweeping up, his father came by to give him a ride home. Since this was the first time he had really seen the dory under construction, he asked Matt a lot of questions. To his surprise his son seemed to have a pretty thorough understanding of what had been done up to this point. Both of them stood staring in silence at the dory for several moments before Matt's father said it was time to go.

The two garboard planks attached

Chapter Six
A RIVETING EXPERIENCE

The crew really worked hard the next week. The garboard planks were finally attached to the boat and several other planks were made ready. Bill worked on constructing the FALSE BOTTOM, which would be attached to the outside of the bottom of the boat. The false bottom is designed to protect the bottom of the boat and give it additional strength. It can easily be replaced if it becomes damaged.

Scott was upstairs sanding the boom when Matt arrived on Friday. What was once nothing more than several strips of wood glued together was now a long cylindrical spar. "It's taken me quite a while to shave off the corners and make this pole somewhat round," Scott said to Matt. "Most of the work was done with a PLANE, which is a tool that has a very sharp blade and is used to take very thin shavings off wood. Now I'm sanding the pole to make it perfectly smooth. I've got a lot more sanding to do so if you care to join me I'd love the help," said Scott.

◄ *A plane*

Sanding the boom

Having had the chance to observe Scott working on the boom the week before, Claude had a pretty good idea of how much work was ahead of her when she was given the assignment of making the MAST. The mast is larger than the boom and is the spar that is STEPPED, or attached vertically, in the boat when the sail is being used. In order for the mast to stand up vertically, it needs to fit securely in place.

After Claude finished rounding off the spar she made a TENON on the end of the mast. The tenon is a small rectangular piece of wood that sticks out like a tongue after the wood surrounding it is cut away. When the mast is stepped, the tenon will fit into a MORTISE which is the rectangular slot that has been cut out of a structure called the MAST STEP. The mast step is designed to hold the mast. When the mast and boom are in place, a sail can be rigged to them so it can be either raised or lowered as needed.

≺ *Planing the mast*

31

Filing the mast tenon

Riveting the planks ➤

While Claude continued to work on the mast, Bill and Scott were busy fitting and attaching the next four planks to the dory. The last plank was being attached when Matt arrived at the end of the week. "These planks are made from very thin strips of wood. They cannot be nailed together the traditional way," Bill explained to Matt. "Instead, the nailing system used is called RIVETING. Riveting the planks sometimes requires two people to work together. One person bangs a special wire nail through one side of the plank and holds it in place while the second person adds a special fastener called a burr to the other side. The burr is put on with a special tool called a rove iron. The shaft of the nail is then snapped off, and the remaining tip pounded flush to the burr."

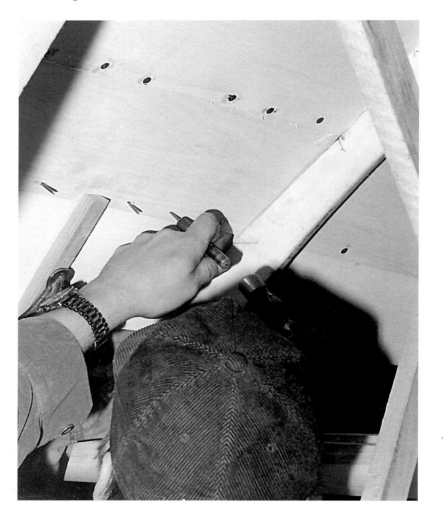

"It sounds a little complicated," Matt said, as he watched them repeat the process all the way down the plank.

"It's not, really," Bill replied. "After the first few you kind of get the hang of it, and then you can work pretty quickly."

When all the students had gone and Matt had finished sweeping, he sat down to wait for his father. His thoughts drifted towards the dory. "What a fine boat this is turning out to be. The people who are going to own this boat when it's all finished are going to be so lucky!"

Wishful thinking ➤

◄ *Riveting view from underneath the boat*

Chapter Seven
ALL STEAMED UP

At the beginning of the next week, Scott was given his assignment to build the TILLER and RUDDER. The tiller is a long stick-like handle, which controls and turns the rudder. The rudder controls the direction of the boat. The rudder and tiller are mounted on a hinge on the transom. Scott seemed to take great pride in working on the tiller, which he made by gluing several long pieces of mahogany together. Once the glue dried, he used a plane to gradually shave the corners off to make them rounded so that the tiller would be comfortable to hold.

The rudder section took Scott quite awhile to build. The first step was cutting out several pieces of plywood and gluing and clamping them together to form the basic shape of the rudder. Then Scott painted an epoxy resin over the rudder to protect the wood, because part of the rudder is submerged in the water. Once the resin hardened, he sanded the whole rudder to make it smooth and ready for painting. The RUDDER CHEEK was then screwed to the rudder. The rudder cheek holds the tiller in place. Small wooden pegs or BUNGS are then tapped into the screw holes of the rudder cheek and later cut with a chisel. A final sanding is then done so that the bungs are flush with the surface.

When he came back at the end of the week, Matt was surprised to see that the dory had been turned right side up. "I'd like to get this SHEER PLANK clamped down. It's the top plank and the last one to be attached. Once we have the sheer plank attached, we will really be able to see the lines and curves of the boat. Maybe you could give me a hand, Matt. A second pair of hands would really be helpful," said Bill.

With the plank in place and the boat righted, Matt's father seemed even

Planing the tiller ➤

37

Clamping the rudder cheek to the rudder

Sanding the rudder ➤

Tapping the wooden bungs into the rudder cheek ≺

Tiller and rudder painted, varnished and ready to go ≻

40

more interested in looking over the boat when he stopped by to pick up his son. "Most of the exterior shell is finished now, and the students are going to be working on strengthening the boat from the inside and adding the finishing touches," Matt explained to his father. "I'm going to stop by on Monday because Bill mentioned that they would be steam bending wood, and he suggested that I might want to see how it is done."

"It certainly does sound interesting," Matt's father said. "It's too bad I have to go to work or I'd come by to watch myself."

The process of steam bending wood is pretty tricky, as Matt found out when he arrived on Monday. The first person he saw outside the school was Claude, kneeling in a pool of mud and steam.

"I'm in charge of keeping an eye on the temperature," Claude explained. "One of these drums has

Getting the water up to temperature to create steam

43

a water-filled coil in it that is being heated by a kerosene-fueled burner. When the water in the coil gets heated high enough, it will convert to steam. The steam will then be channeled from the coil into a plastic pipe. Once the pipe is filled with steam we will place a bundle of oak ribs in the pipe and seal it at both ends. The temperature in the pipe must be approximately 205 degrees. The wood will remain in the pipe for about 20 minutes where it absorbs moisture from the steam. The process softens the wood so that it becomes flexible and doesn't snap when it is bent. The wood that is in the pipe now is just about ready to be taken out, so get ready to follow me," Claude said.

Before Matt could say anything, Claude had opened the pipe, pulled out a rib and had run with it into the school. Scott and Dave were waiting at the boat and immediately placed the rib in position, clamping and hammering it so that it conformed to the shape of the boat.

"It's important to work quickly with wood that has been steamed," Dave told Matt. "Once the wood starts to cool off it loses the ability to bend. I'm sure that out of the 14 ribs that are going to be attached several will snap in the process. But I guess that's why I love boat building. It's a real challenge!"

Matt watched until the last rib had been hammered into place. "The boat has gained a lot of structural strength with the addition of the ribs," Dave said. "Now the students will spend the rest of the week measuring and fitting some of the interior structures. There are many pieces to add, but now we will be moving along at a rapid pace."

"I think I'll come back before the end of the week," Matt said. "I really don't want to miss anything."

When Matt returned, Claude was ready to attach the two RISERS to the boat. "The risers are long narrow pieces of wood that have been contoured to run from

Loading the oak ribs into the pipe to steam

Riveting the steam-bent ribs to the planks

45

the bow frame to the stern frame and are designed to support the seats in the boat," Claude told Matt. "If you hold one piece in place for me, I can drill the screw holes. Just try to hold it in the exact spot."

"This isn't as easy as it looks," Matt said as he struggled to keep the first riser in position. After he finished helping Claude, Matt looked around the shop and saw that the floor was covered with wood shavings. Since the students were busy trying to get the boat ready for its launching in two weeks, Matt thought they would appreciate some extra help cleaning up.

Some extra help ➤

◄ *Attaching the risers*

Chapter Eight
THE COUNTDOWN

At the end of the week Matt returned to find that the interior of the boat had been painted and that the RUB RAILS had been attached. The rub rail is a narrow strip of wood that is attached to the top plank along the outside edge to make it more rigid and to protect the plank from anything rubbing up against it. The top side of the plank is called the GUNWALE. On further inspection Matt saw that the centerboard trunk case was also now attached and in place.

After Matt finished sweeping the floor, Dave asked him if he had time to vacuum the inside of the boat. Some of the students were returning over the weekend to put on a second coat of paint, and all the dust had to be removed before they could begin. The countdown had now begun. The launching was to take place next Saturday.

During the final week of construction, Bill, Scott and Claude spent long hours at the boat school. The mahogany seats and floorboards were fitted and installed with great care. There were many small pieces that were added to the dory that required a lot of time and patience to make. To produce a first-class boat that is both functional and beautiful, the students could not allow themselves to rush through the final details. Each surface of the boat had to be sanded and painted or varnished several times in order to achieve a smooth-as-glass finish.

With the finishing touches being added, Matt and his father began to stop by the school almost every day to see the progress. "There has been a great deal of pride put into the workmanship of this boat," Matt's father said as he walked around the boat, lightly touching it.

Matt thought about what his father had said. "I wonder if the owners will

Vacuuming out the dust in preparation for the second coat of paint ➢

really appreciate this boat? Tomorrow is the launching and I know the owners will be there. In a way I feel a little uneasy about meeting them."

"Don't worry about it, son," said Matt's father. "I have a feeling that the owners of this boat are probably very special people. I'm sure they will take good care of her."

Matt just couldn't sleep that night. Although the boat launching wasn't scheduled until noon, he knew Claude, Bill and Scott would be down at the shop at the crack of dawn inspecting the dory one final time and doing last-minute preparations for its maiden voyage that afternoon. Also, because Christmas was just one week away, the students had decided to decorate the boats, and Matt had agreed to help before the launching.

Seats and a section of the floorboards installed ➢

◄ *Attaching the seats*

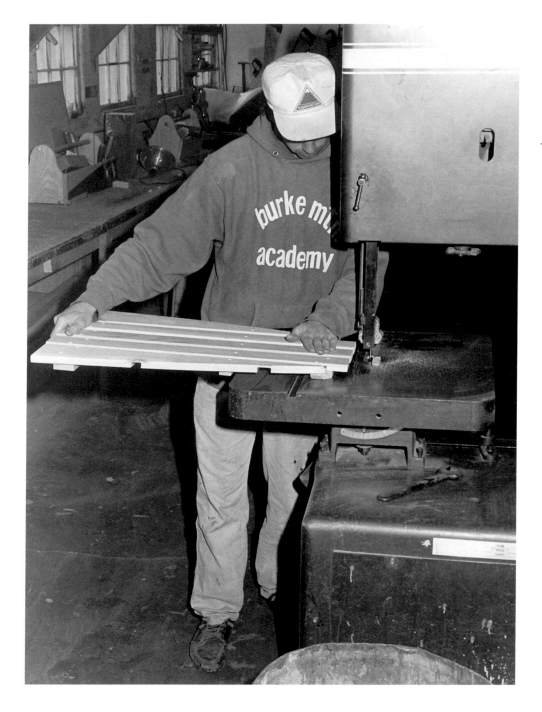

Sawing a section of the floorboards for a perfect fit

Installing the final section of the floorboards ➢

A view of the boat upside down. The false bottom is attached and the final coat of paint is applied

Dory with mast and boom ➤

Chapter Nine
AN ENVELOPE

When daylight finally came, Matt quietly dressed and left his parents a note telling them that he had gone over to the shop and that he would meet them there later. The night before both Matt's parents had told him how proud they were of him for sticking to his commitment at the boat school. They also said that they were planning to attend the launching. His mother suggested that Matt wear plenty of warm clothes because the weather forecast called for zero-degree temperatures and high winds. Matt's mother was right. It was a cold winter's morning, but the chilling temperatures weren't a concern for Matt this morning.

A hard frost covered the ground as Matt jogged all the way to the boat school. When Matt arrived at the school, there weren't any cars parked outside so he knew that no one had arrived yet. Luckily, the side door hadn't been locked the night before so he slipped into the dimly lit building. As Matt gazed around, he realized how quiet and peaceful the shop seemed. He stood alone looking at the Christmas tree, and then his eyes wandered over to the dories that would be launched that day.

As he walked closer to the boat that he had worked on, he noticed something odd. Not only did the dory have a large wreath over its bow, but it also had a large red ribbon and bow tied around it as if it had been wrapped up like a Christmas present. When he bent down to look at the bow, his eyes focused on an envelope that was resting on the boat. The envelope had his name on it. A huge smile spread over his face. Matt slowly picked up the envelope and opened it. It seemed too good to be true! Perhaps he was dreaming. Yes, this was a Christmas present for someone! Now Matt realized why his father had seemed so confident when he assured him that this boat would always be appreciated and well taken care of.

By noontime the shop had filled up with a crowd of cheerful people who had come to see the launching. The atmosphere was very festive as families and friends of the students walked around the boats admiring their beauty and craftsmanship. When the ceremony began, all the boat school students, instructors and new boat owners were introduced. Claude was given the honor of christening the boat she had worked on so hard. "I christen thee *DORY GLORY*," she said. "May all those who venture to sea with her be blessed." Then she lifted up the customary bottle of champagne and proceeded to smash it over the bow of the boat. Everyone cheered and clapped.

After all the other boats had been christened, they were carried out of the shop by the students, who had truly learned to work together as a team. Once outside, the students lifted the boats onto boat trailers,

Christening the dory with champagne ➤

58

which were then hauled to the nearby river. Usually, the tradition that is followed at the boat school is to have the new owner take the finished boat out on its maiden voyage. Unfortunately, because the weather had turned so rough, the instructors decided that it would be too dangerous to permit anyone to go out on the water.

However, everyone agreed that lowering the dory into the water and keeping it close to shore would certainly be permissible. And, although he was slightly disappointed just sitting with both oars resting in the water, Matt couldn't help but begin to dream about the adventures that would surely lie ahead.

The Maiden Voyage! ➤

Chapter Ten
A ROUND OF APPLAUSE

With the weekend festivities over, Matt greeted Monday morning with some reluctance. Back at school now, he could barely concentrate knowing that at 10:15 a.m. he would be going to his third-period class to give his independent project presentation.

When the time came, Matt meandered his way down to his class. He entered the room and found that his teacher had already asked the class to quiet down and had explained that Matt would be giving a short presentation. Matt took a deep breath and slowly walked to the front of the room.

Matt cleared his throat and decided to ignore the butterflies that seemed to be dancing in his stomach. He began by telling the class how he first found the boat school. Without skipping a beat he then explained how he was offered a job and how he spent the next four months watching and helping build the dory that was now his. As he continued speaking, he became less and less anxious. This was a new experience for Matt. He went on to give a detailed description of the construction of the dory and even had to stop occasionally to answer questions from his classmates.

To assist in his presentation, Matt used the white board in front of the room to draw a picture of the boat. He also handed out a boat building vocabulary list to each student. Matt held up one photograph that his mother had taken of him sitting in the dory on the day of the launching and said that he regretted not taking pictures of the boat as it was being built. Photographs of the construction would have been a great way for students to learn about boat building.

The students in Matt's class were very impressed with the knowledge that

Matt had gained. He really seemed to be an expert on the subject. They were also somewhat in awe of the fact that Matt had been working alongside the older students at the boat school. When Matt concluded his presentation, he received a round of applause that made him feel pretty good, but not as good as the A+ that his teacher gave him for his presentation.

Preparing for his independent study presentation, keeping up with his other school work and working at the boat school had kept Matt very busy. He was really ready for Christmas break. Now he would have time to think about all the great fishing he would be able to do aboard *DORY GLORY*. Since fishing can be a very expensive hobby, Matt was glad that he had saved all the money he had earned at the boat school. During this vacation he could spend endless hours reading fishing magazines and perusing the big fat fishing catalogues that he had piled up in his room. One could never have too many fishing rods or reels!

School vacation flew by quickly, but Matt didn't mind all that much. He enjoyed his time off, but he was also looking forward to spring. Although school was still a real challenge, Matt returned from vacation with a little more confidence. On his first day back at school Matt decided to walk home when school let out. After sitting in class all day, the cold fresh air felt wonderful, and since he really didn't have any special plans, he thought he would try taking a different route home. After all, unless you have been down a road before, you can never really be sure where it will lead you.

MATT'S LIST of Boat Building Terms

BATTENS   *flexible strips of wood which are used in lofting to help draw the curved lines of the boat*

BOOM   *a horizontal spar to which the bottom of the sail can be attached*

BOW   *the front end of the boat*

BRIGHTWORK   *the wood on a boat that is left unpainted and often finished with varnish*

BUNGS   *wooden plugs used to fill screw holes*

CENTERBOARD   *the movable rectangular board which can be raised or lowered into the water from a slot in the bottom to help keep a boat steady when it is under sail*

CENTERBOARD TRUNK CASE   *holds the center-board in place*

FALSE BOTTOM   *the removable floor on a boat which protects the bottom of the boat*

GARBOARD PLANK   *the first bottom plank of the hull*

GUNWALE   *the top edge of the sheer plank*

HULL   *the body of the boat*

LOFTING   *drawing the full-size plans of the boat*

MAST   *the vertical spar that can be rigged with a sail*

MAST STEP   *a structure that holds the mast in place*

MORTISE   *a slot cut out of a piece of wood which is designed to have another piece of wood (See TENON) fit into it*

PLANE   *a woodworking tool which is used to shave pieces of wood.*

PLANKS   *the wooden siding of a boat*

RIBS   *the frames of a boat that help to make it sturdy*

RIB FRAME   *sections of wood which when attached to the bottom act as the skeleton of the boat and provide a surface to which the planks are attached*

RISER   *the board that runs from stem to stern and supports the seats*

RIVET   *the method of nailing planks on a boat*

RUB RAIL   *a narrow strip of wood or metal that is attached to the outside of the sheer plank and is level with the gunwale*

RUDDER   *a wide piece of wood which is attached at the stern on hinges and is used to turn or change the boat's direction*

RUDDER CHEEK   *located at the top of the rudder, it holds the tiller*

SCARPH   *the process of tapering two pieces of wood so they overlap when they are joined to form one piece*

SHEER PLANK   *the top plank that shows the curved lines of the boat*

SPAR   *a pole which can function as a mast or boom*

STEM   *the front of the boat where the two sides meet*

STEP   *standing the mast up and securing it*

STERN   *the back end of the boat*

STRONGBACK   *the structure that supports the boat during construction*

TENON   *a tongue-like stub that sticks out at the end of a piece of lumber after the wood around it has been cut away, in order to fit perfectly into a slot (See MORTISE) which has been made to receive it*

TILLER   *a horizontal handle that turns the rudder*

TRANSOM   *the flat stern end section of the hull*

MATT'S DRAWING

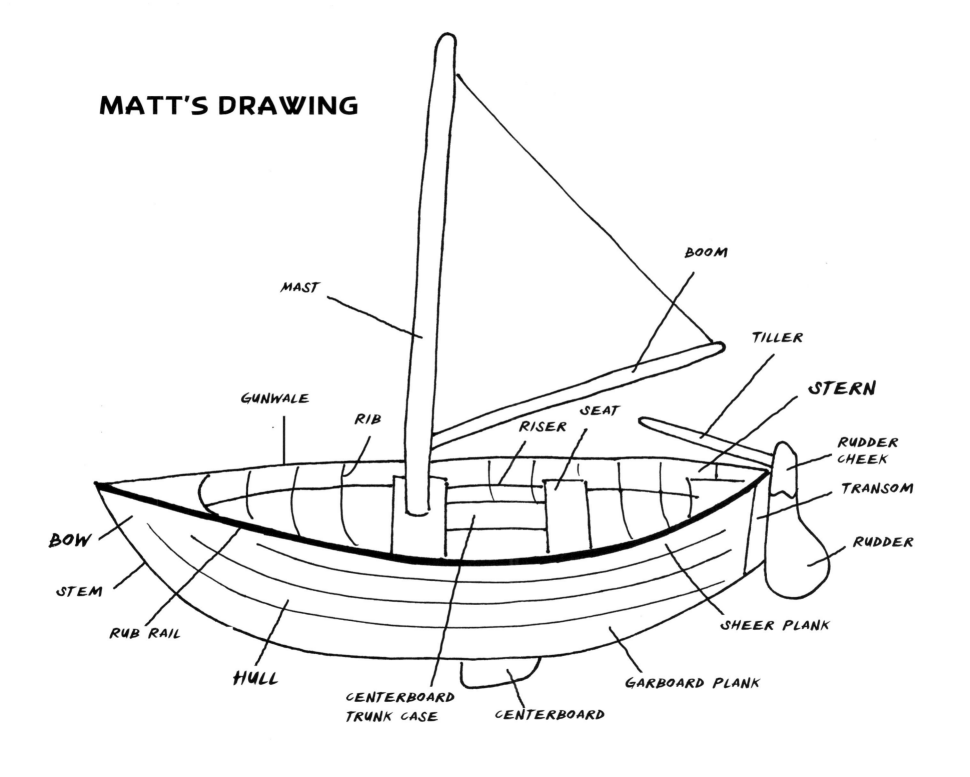

BOOM

MAST

TILLER

STERN

GUNWALE

RIB

RISER   SEAT

RUDDER
CHEEK

TRANSOM

RUDDER

BOW

STEM

SHEER PLANK

RUB RAIL

HULL

CENTERBOARD
TRUNK CASE

CENTERBOARD

GARBOARD PLANK